The LAST FIREHAWK

The Crystal Caverns

by
Katrina Charman
illustrated by
Jeremy Norton

BRANCHES

SCHOLASTIC INC.

The LAST FIREHAWK

Read All the Books

1 The Ember Stone

2 The Crystal Caverns

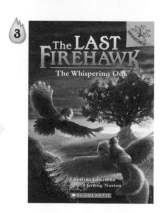

3 The Whispering Oak

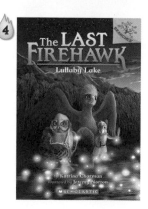

4 Lullaby Lake

Table of Contents

For Maddie, Piper, and Riley. —KC
Thank you to my parents, who showed me the value of art. —JN

Text copyright © 2017 by Katrina Charman
Illustrations by Jeremy Norton copyright © 2017 by Scholastic Inc.

All rights reserved. Published by Scholastic Inc., *Publishers since 1920.*
SCHOLASTIC, BRANCHES, and associated logos are trademarks
and/or registered trademarks of Scholastic Inc.

The publisher does not have any control over and does not assume any responsibility for author or third-party websites or their content.

Library of Congress Cataloging-in-Publication Data

Names: Charman, Katrina, author. | Norton, Jeremy, illustrator.
Title: The crystal caverns / by Katrina Charman.
Description: First edition. | New York, NY : Branches/Scholastic Inc., 2017.| Series: The last firehawk ; 2 | Summary: Tag the owl, Skyla the squirrel, and Blaze the newly hatched firehawk, journey north to the Crystal Caverns searching for the next piece of the magical Ember Stone—but the evil vulture Thorn is also after the stone, and his ice leopards are close behind the heroes.
Identifiers: LCCN 2016054930 | ISBN 9781338122510 (pbk. : alk. paper) | ISBN 9781338122527 (hardcover : alk. paper)
Subjects: LCSH: Owls—Juvenile fiction. | Squirrels—Juvenile fiction. | Animals, Mythical—Juvenile fiction. | Magic—Juvenile fiction. | Quests (Expeditions)—Juvenile fiction. | Adventure stories. | CYAC: Owls—Fiction. | Squirrels—Fiction. | Animals, Mythical—Fiction. | Magic—Fiction. | Fantasy. | GSAFD: Adventure fiction. | LCGFT: Action and adventure fiction.
Classification: LCC PZ7.1.C495 Cr 2017 | DDC [Fic]—dc23 LC record available at https://lccn.loc.gov/2016054930

10 9 8 7 6 5 4 3 2 1   17 18 19 20 21

Printed in China   38
First edition, December 2017
Edited by Katie Carella
Book design by Maria Mercado

~ INTRODUCTION ~

In the enchanted land of Perodia,
lies Valor Wood—a forest filled with magic and
light. There, a wise owl named Grey leads the
Owls of Valor. These brave warriors protect the
creatures of the wood. But a darkness is spreading
across Perodia . . .

A powerful old vulture called Thorn wants to
destroy Perodia. He controls The Shadow—a dark
magic. Whenever The Shadow appears, Thorn
and his army of orange-eyed spies are nearby.

Tag, a small barn owl, has set off to find the
lost pieces of the Ember Stone. Tag hopes this
magical stone will be strong enough to stop Thorn
once and for all. Tag and his friend Skyla have
weapons, armor, and a magical map. They also
have Blaze—the last firehawk—on their side. But
their journey has only just begun . . .

TO THE NORTH

Tag, Skyla, and Blaze stood on a golden, sandy beach. The water was so blue, it sparkled in the sunlight.

Tag studied the magical map.

Skyla pointed to BLUE BAY at the bottom of the map. "We are here," she said.

Tag nodded and pulled a piece of purple stone from his sack: the Ember Stone. It felt warm in his wing.

Tag laid the stone on the map. A spot glowed brightly at the very top.

"The next piece of the Ember Stone is at the Crystal Caverns," Skyla said.

"It looks like one day's journey," Tag said.

"Peep!" Blaze tapped her beak on a long, zig-zaggy line on the paper.

"The Jagged Mountains," Skyla read. "Yes, Blaze, we will have to cross those."

"Thorn's spies are everywhere," Tag told them. "We should fly. We'll move faster."

"Um, squirrels can't fly," Skyla said.

Tag grinned. "You can ride on Blaze's back!"

"Fly!" Blaze said. "Fly!"

Tag and Skyla stared at Blaze.

"Blaze's first word!" Tag smiled.

"Fly!" Blaze said again. Her gold, red, and orange wings suddenly burst into flame.

Tag gasped.

"Whoa! Looks like Blaze has learned more than a new word!" Skyla said. "Tag, can the fire hurt her?"

Tag shook his head. "Fire can't hurt Blaze. Remember what Grey told us? She's a firehawk. She was born in flame."

Tag turned to Blaze. "We can't let Thorn's spies find out about your new power. Thorn already wants to capture you to lead him to the Ember Stone. He could try to use your power against Perodia."

Skyla nodded. "Tag's right, Blaze. We need to keep your fire power hidden."

Blaze flapped her wings, but the flames wouldn't go out.

Tag and Skyla scooped water into large shells. They threw it over Blaze. Steam rose from her dripping wet feathers.

Blaze gave a little peep.

Suddenly, a large gray cloud moved across the bay. It covered the sun.

"Dark!" Blaze cried.

"The Shadow!" Tag yelled. "We need to leave!"

"But I can't ride on Blaze's back!" Skyla cried. "I'll be a sizzled squirrel!"

"It's the only way," Tag told her. "I'm too small to carry you. We have to get to the Crystal Caverns before Thorn's spies find us."

"Promise your wings won't catch on fire again?" Skyla asked Blaze, as she climbed onto her back.

Blaze nodded. "Peep!"

Tag tucked the map and stone inside his sack. Then the three friends flew north as fast as they could.

CHAPTER 2

THE JAGGED MOUNTAINS

The sun had started to set as Tag and Blaze landed softly in the snow. They had flown all day without stopping. Now they stood at the bottom of a tall mountain.

"We've reached the Jagged Mountains," Tag said.

"We flew so fast," Skyla said, jumping off Blaze's back. "I bet Thorn is waaaay behind us!"

"There's no sign of The Shadow," Tag agreed, shivering. "But a storm is coming."

HOOOOOOWOOOOOO! The wind howled. Snowflakes swirled above them.

Skyla rubbed her paws together. "It's so cold!" she said. She wrapped her thick tail around herself.

Tag looked at the mountain. "The Crystal Caverns must be on the other side of this," he said.

"No fly?" Blaze asked, as the wind blew harder.

"No, Blaze," Tag said. "We can't fly—not through this storm."

"We could camp here until it's over?" Skyla suggested.

Tag shook his head. "We have to keep moving."

He looked up. The mountain was so tall, it disappeared beneath the clouds. "We will have to climb."

"To the top?!" Skyla squeaked.

Tag patted his sack to make sure the stone was safe. "We have to find the next piece of the Ember Stone before Thorn finds *us*."

The friends started the steep climb up the mountainside. The snow fell fast as they climbed higher, until they could hardly see.

"B-b-b-blaze," Skyla said, her teeth chattering. "Could your fire keep us warm?"

"Peep!" said Blaze.

"The clouds should hide your firelight, but don't let your wings get too bright," Tag warned Blaze.

Blaze thought for a moment, then nodded. Her wings began to glow. Her fiery feathers got warmer and brighter.

Soon, Tag and Skyla started to warm up.

The three friends pushed on through the storm.

Finally, they reached the top of the Jagged Mountains.

Tag dropped his sack.

The sky was clear. The moon was full and bright.

"You can see the whole of Perodia from here!" Skyla said.

Blaze ruffled her feathers. "Peep!" she cried, pointing her beak into the distance.

The land to the north glowed white as far as the eye could see. In the very middle, rose a huge, sparkly diamond.

Tag grinned at his friends. "We've found the Crystal Caverns!"

THE CRYSTAL CAVERNS

Tag soared down the mountain. Blaze followed—with Skyla clinging to her back.

They soon landed on the cool, glassy ice below.

Five huge ice caverns loomed ahead of them in a semi-circle. Small, dirty mounds of snow surrounded the caverns.

Glittering snowflakes fell from the sky.

Skyla stuck out her tongue to catch one. "These snowflakes are as soft as feathers!" she giggled.

Blaze squawked, snapping at snowflakes with her beak.

Tag looked at the caverns, hoping that the next piece of the Ember Stone would be easy to find.

Suddenly, Skyla cried out, "Eek!"

"Skyla?" Tag called.

Skyla had disappeared.

Blaze peeped at a hole in the snow where Skyla had been standing a moment before.

Tag flew to Blaze's side and peered down inside.

"I'm stuck!" Skyla yelled from the deep hole. She tried to climb out, but the snow crumbled in her paws.

Tag reached down. "Grab my wing."

He took Skyla's paw and groaned as he pulled as hard as he could.

Blaze held onto Tag's tail feathers and helped him pull.

Skyla finally broke free and the friends landed in a jumble of feathers and fur.

"Thanks, guys!" Skyla said. She brushed snow from her tail, then hugged Tag and Blaze.

Tag felt a prickle down his neck, as though someone was watching.

"I think we are being followed," he whispered. "Let's keep moving."

Skyla searched the sky for Thorn's spies. "I'll keep an eye out for tiger bats," she said.

"Don't forget prickle ants," Tag added, looking at the ground.

"Peep!" Blaze agreed, stamping her feet.

Thorn's spies, Tag thought with a shiver. *Tiger bats, prickle ants. What other dark creatures could be out here?*

Skyla pointed to the five caverns. "So which cavern holds the Ember Stone?" she asked.

"I don't know, but the magical map should show us the way," Tag said. He unrolled the map and took out the piece of stone.

Tag frowned. "That's strange . . . the stone feels cold."

"Why isn't its magic working?" Skyla asked.

Tag sat on one of the small, dirty mounds of snow to think.

"I'm not sure," Tag replied. "But Blaze should be able to lead us to the next piece of the stone. Blaze, can you help?"

Blaze nodded.

Tag watched as Blaze hopped over to the caverns. She peered inside each one in turn. Then she stood in front of the largest cavern in the middle.

"Peep!" she cried.

"I think Blaze wants to try that one," Skyla said.

Tag looked at the biggest cavern.

Before he could say anything, the mound beneath him suddenly moved!

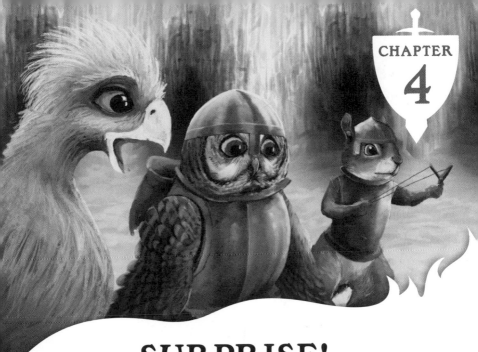

SURPRISE!

Tag jumped up. Behind him, another snow mound moved, then another.

"What's happening?" Skyla cried. She pulled out her slingshot as the snow rumbled and crumbled around her.

Blaze snapped her beak at the snow.

Then a large head popped up out of one of the mounds.

It was a huge, spotted black-and-grey seal!
"Can we help you?" the seal boomed.
Blaze covered her ears. The sound echoed around the caverns as hundreds more seals popped up out of the snow.

The black-and-grey seal shuffled toward them. His long white whiskers shook as he moved.

"Wh-wh-who are you?" Skyla squeaked.

"I'm Gilbert," the seal said. He waved his flipper.

Tag checked Gilbert's eyes. They were black. "Did Thorn send you?" Tag asked.

Gilbert blinked. "Who is Thorn?"

"You haven't heard of Thorn?" Skyla asked.

Gilbert shook his head. "We don't get many visitors. You are the first animals we've seen in a long time." He looked closely at Blaze. "Although . . . I think I've seen someone like *you* before."

"Peep!" Blaze cried.

"You've seen a firehawk?" Skyla asked.

Gilbert nodded at Skyla. "Are you a groundhog?" he asked. "I've always wanted to meet a groundhog."

"Ha! Ha! Ha!" Skyla fell to the ground, howling with laughter.

"Skyla is a squirrel," Tag explained. "I'm Tag and I'm an owl. One day, I will be an Owl of Valor."

"This is Blaze," Tag continued. "The last firehawk."

"That sounds important," said Gilbert.

Tag showed Gilbert the piece of the Ember Stone. It was still cold. "Have you seen anything like this before?" he asked.

Gilbert shook his head.

"We think there's one just like it hidden inside here," Skyla said, pointing to the largest cavern.

"Oh no!" cried Gilbert. "Don't go in there. If you do, you won't come out."

"Peep?" asked Blaze.

"It's too dangerous," Gilbert said. "Years ago, a young seal named Coralie went inside."

"What happened to her?" asked Tag.

"We never saw her again," Gilbert replied.

WAAAAAAHHHHHH!

A loud wailing noise came from the big cavern.

Tag pulled out his dagger.

"Maybe we should wait until morning . . ." Skyla said, moving closer to Tag. "We could eat and rest tonight."

"Is it safe here?" Tag asked Gilbert.

"We'll keep you safe," Gilbert told him. He called more seals over. They quickly got to work, building a snow circle to hide the three friends.

Then the seals buried themselves back down inside their snow mounds.

"We'll go into the cavern as soon as it's light out," Tag told Skyla and Blaze.

WAAAAAAHHHHHH!

Skyla jumped at the noise. "Do we really have to go in there?" she asked.

"We've got no choice," Tag told her. "We have to find the next piece of the Ember Stone. All of Perodia is counting on us."

INTO THE MAZE

Tag woke early the next morning. He checked that the stone was safe inside his sack. Then he woke Skyla and Blaze.

"Time to go," he whispered.

"We should make a plan," Skyla suggested, "to make sure we don't get lost in this ice cavern just like that little seal named Coralie."

"Peep!" Blaze agreed.

Tag pulled out a wingful of Skyla's acorns from his sack. "We could use these to mark our way."

"I might need those for battle—if Thorn's spies show up," Skyla said. "Can we use berries instead?"

"Okay," Tag said, jumping over a sleeping seal. "So, if we get turned around, we'll just follow the berries back to the exit."

"Dark!" Blaze cried, looking up. "Dark! Dark!"

A black cloud filled the sky.

"The Shadow!" Tag shouted.

As The Shadow moved slowly toward them in the distance, the sparkling white ice below turned black.

"Let's go!" Skyla yelled.

Blaze stood still. "Peep!" she cried, pointing her beak at the sleeping seals.

"They will be safe hidden beneath the snow," Tag told her.

The three friends ran inside the largest cavern.

As they walked, Skyla placed berries on the icy floor to mark their route.

"It's like we're in a giant maze of mirrors!" Tag said, walking along the shiny hallways. He could see his reflection in the floor and in the walls.

The friends stopped at the end of the path. It split into two.

"Which way, Blaze?" Tag asked.

Blaze hopped along one path, then shook her head. She returned to hop down the other.

"Is it this way?" Skyla asked.

Blaze nodded. "Peep!"

Tag and Skyla followed Blaze down the winding path. Twisting and turning, up and down, left and right, until Tag stopped suddenly.

"Wait! We've been this way before," Tag said. He pointed to the berries on the ground.

Skyla sighed. "Maybe Blaze doesn't know the way after all?"

Blaze stamped her feet. "Peep!" she cried.

Tag patted Blaze on the wing. "I'm sorry, Blaze," he said. "This can't be the right way."

They turned around to head back the way they came.

Tag paused. "There are already berries on this path, too," he said.

"Peep!" Blaze said, holding up a berry in her beak.

They walked until they found another path that split into two.

"There are berries here, too!" Skyla said. "How are there berries on *every* path?"

Tag frowned. "I think we've been walking in circles! We must be lost."

"Lost!" Blaze peeped. Skyla hugged her.

"How will we find our way out?" Skyla asked Tag.

Tag shook his head slowly. "I am not sure . . ." he said, thinking about the little seal. *Coralie was lost forever. Who will save Perodia if we're lost forever, too?*

THE LOST SEAL

Tag, Skyla, and Blaze faced two paths leading in different directions. Each path had a trail of berries on it. And the trail behind them was covered already, too. They didn't know which way to go.

WAAAAAHHHHH!

Tag froze at the wailing sound. It was the same sound from last night—but louder now.

Skyla pulled out her slingshot.

Blaze flapped her wings. They started to glow.

"Careful, Blaze!" Tag warned her. "Your fire power would melt the ice."

"Then we'd really be in trouble!" Skyla said.

Blaze stood very still.

WAAAAAHHHHH!

The sound rang out again.

"I think we should head *away* from that scary sound," said Skyla.

"But maybe that noise is being made by someone—or something—guarding the Ember Stone," Tag argued.

Blaze hopped down the path where the cry sounded the loudest.

"It looks like Blaze agrees with me," Tag told Skyla.

"Fine!" Skyla huffed. "But I'm keeping my slingshot loaded just in case."

Blaze led the way.

Soon, the friends turned a corner.

"Hey!" Skyla said, looking at the icy floor. "There are no more berries—we haven't been this way before."

WAAAAAAHHHHH!

"The noise is louder than ever!" Tag said, moving faster. "We must be getting close!"

The friends rounded another corner. The path opened up into a large cave. In the center, they saw a small spotted seal sitting on a large chunk of ice.

WAAAAAAHHHHH!

The seal saw Tag, Skyla, and Blaze and gasped. "I am saved!" the seal shouted, wiping away her tears.

Skyla's tail stood up. "You must be Coralie—the lost seal!" she exclaimed.

"Yes," Coralie said. "I'd just wanted to explore—the sparkly caverns were so beautiful—but I couldn't find my way out."

Coralie sniffed. "How did you find me?"

"We heard your cry and followed it," Skyla said.

"I was calling for help," Coralie said. "I've been so lonely."

Tag looked around. All he could see was ice. "What do you eat?" he asked Coralie.

"I'll show you," she replied. Coralie used her teeth to break a hole in the ice floor.

"Fish!" Skyla cried, as a silver fish swam past.

Coralie scooped it up in a flash, and gulped it down.

"Sorry," she mumbled. "Did you want some? I'm not used to having company."

Skyla crinkled her nose. "No, thank you," she said.

"So, how do we get out?" Coralie asked.

Tag sighed. "We're lost, too. Our map only showed us the way in, not the way out."

As Tag pulled out Grey's map, the purple piece of the Ember Stone fell to the floor.

Blaze quickly scooped it up.

Coralie's eyes widened. "How did you get that out of the ice?" she asked.

"Wait," Skyla replied. "You've seen this stone before?"

Coralie examined the stone. "Yes . . . or one just like it. The one I know is bigger."

Tag bounced up and down. "Can you take us to it?" he asked.

Coralie looked at the friends. "Sure. It's not far—as long as you can swim."

CHAPTER 7

THE HIDDEN CAVE

Coralie led Tag, Skyla, and Blaze through an icy tunnel to a large hole in the ice.

Skyla dipped a toe in the water. "It's f-f-freezing!" she cried.

"We have to swim *below the ice*?" Tag asked.

"Yes, there's another tunnel underneath," Coralie said. "It leads to a hidden cave."

"That's where you saw the stone?" Skyla asked.

Coralie nodded. "It's not far," she told them. "A quick dip under the water and then we'll pop back up on the other side."

"We can't really swim . . ." Tag said, looking at his friends.

Coralie stroked her whiskers. "You could ride on my back?" she suggested.

Tag looked at Skyla and Blaze. *Can all three of us fit on Coralie's back?*

"Swim!" Blaze peeped.

SPLASH! Blaze dove into the water. She disappeared beneath the ice.

Skyla's jaw dropped.

"I guess firehawks can swim after all!" Tag said.

Coralie grinned. "Ready?"

"I hate getting wet," Skyla grumbled.

"Remember," Tag said, "it's just a dip."

Tag climbed onto Coralie's back. Skyla followed, holding tightly to the seal's slick fur.

"Hold your breath," Coralie told them.

They took a deep breath and closed their eyes.

Coralie dove into the freezing water.

After a few seconds, Coralie swam up into the hidden cave.

Tag shook icy droplets from his wings as he gazed around the small, glittery cave.

"This cave is so beautiful!" Skyla said, squeezing water out of her tail.

"Ow!" Tag cried suddenly. "The sack is burning me!"

Tag threw down the sack. It slid along the ice and stopped at the wall.

The four friends hurried over, and peered inside as Tag carefully opened the sack.

"Look!" Skyla yelled. "Our stone is glowing!"

"And it's definitely hot again!" Tag said.

"Peep! Peep! Peep!" Blaze said. She pecked at the icy wall.

"What is it, Blaze?" Tag asked.

Something glowed deep inside the wall of ice. The light grew brighter and brighter—until the whole cavern sparkled purple.

Tag gasped. "It's the next piece of the Ember Stone!"

FIRE POWER!

The friends stared at the purple stone. It looked like it was floating in the ice.

"I've never seen it glow before!" Coralie said, shielding her eyes.

"The Ember Stone is magical," Tag explained. "It must know that our piece of the stone is nearby."

"Wow!" Coralie breathed.

"How are we going to get it out of the ice?" Skyla asked.

Tag put a wing on the ice wall. It was as thick as he was tall. *We're going to need something really strong to break through this*, he thought.

Then Tag remembered something: Grey had told them that a firehawk's cry could be used as a weapon. Tag had seen proof of this when Blaze's cry had saved them from a tiger bat attack in Valor Wood.

Tag turned to Blaze. "Do you think you could use your cry to crack open the ice wall?" he asked.

Blaze nodded.

"Stand back," Tag told Skyla and Coralie. The three friends covered their ears. "Peeeeeeeeep!" Blaze called.

Tag frowned. "Good try, Blaze, but that didn't sound nearly as loud as your cry in Valor Wood."

"Try again," Skyla told her. "As loud as you can."

Blaze opened her beak wide. "Peeeep!" She shook her head. Her cry would not come.

"That's okay, Blaze," Tag said. "You're still learning how your powers work. We'll think of something else."

"Maybe I can dig the stone out?" Skyla said. She scratched at the ice with her sharp claws. They barely made a dent.

"Let me try," Tag said. He pulled out his golden dagger. *There's nothing sharper than this blade,* Tag thought. He attacked the ice until his wing hurt, but he was no closer to the stone.

Skyla's tail drooped. "We'll never reach it!"

Tag looked at Blaze again. "Grey told us that only a firehawk could find the Ember Stone . . ."

"Yes," Skyla agreed. "But her cry isn't working."

"We have no choice," he said. "Blaze will have to use her fire power."

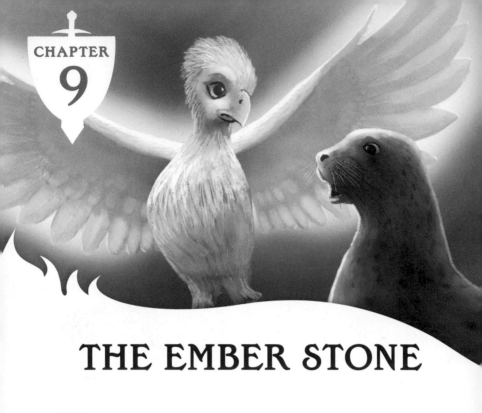

THE EMBER STONE

Blaze gently moved her wings up and down. Her feathers began to glow.

Coralie stared at Blaze. "Is Blaze magical, too?"

Tag nodded. "Blaze and the Ember Stone are linked somehow. And, yes, her feathers can turn to fire."

"Fire?" Coralie trembled. "The ice cave will melt!"

"Not if Blaze is careful," Tag said. He turned to Blaze. "Do you think you can control your fire power this time?"

"Peep!" Blaze said loudly.

Skyla frowned. "Blaze's fire power is very strong, Tag. She's young. She's still getting used to her powers."

"She can do it," Tag said. "We have to trust her."

"Just keep your flames focused on that wall, Blaze," Skyla said.

"Everyone, stand back!" Tag ordered.

Tag, Skyla, and Coralie stepped away from Blaze and the ice wall.

Blaze flapped her wings. Slowly at first, then faster. Feather by feather, her wings lit up. They glowed red and orange and yellow.

Blaze touched the wall of ice with her flaming wings.

"It's working!" Tag cried. The ice began melting into a watery puddle.

Blaze pushed her shaky wings into the ice. Closer and closer to the next piece of the Ember Stone.

"You're almost there!" Skyla said, jumping up and down.

"You can do it, Blaze!" Tag shouted.

The flames rose higher and higher. The tip of Blaze's wing almost touched the stone . . . Suddenly, she pulled away.

"Peep!" Blaze cried. Her feathers exploded with bright light.

"She's losing control!" Tag shouted. "The cave is melting!"

Skyla hurried closer to Blaze. "Stay calm," she whispered.

Blaze flapped her fiery wings, trying to put out the flames, but they burned even stronger.

"Oh no! The ceiling!" Coralie cried.

Water dripped onto Tag's head. The walls were shifting. Cracks shot across the floor.

"Blaze, quick! Jump into the water!" Tag cried.

Blaze turned and dove into the cold water. Her feathers sizzled. Then she dove deeper, to return to the main cavern.

Skyla jumped onto Coralie's back. "Come on, Tag!" she shouted. "We have to get out of here! We have to follow Blaze!"

"I can't leave without the stone!" Tag yelled, racing toward it.

Just then, the floor split open.

CHAPTER 10

IT'S A TRAP!

Tag swooped into the air before he was pulled underwater by the crumbling ice. He ducked and dove as ice chunks fell all around him.

"Watch out!" Skyla and Coralie yelled from the water.

Tag thrust his right wing into the slushy cave wall, then used his sharp talons to grip the stone.

"It's stuck!" he cried.

"Hurry!" Skyla shouted.

Tag pulled as hard as he could. Finally, the stone came free, but then it slipped from Tag's damp wing!

The stone fell onto a floating chunk of ice. It was out of Tag's reach. The stone slowly slid toward the freezing water when—

Skyla leaped up, dove onto the ice, and caught the stone in her paw!

Tag gasped. "That was close!"

"Let's go!" Skyla told Tag.

Tag jumped onto Coralie's back. They all took a deep breath and ducked under the water.

Soon, the four friends were back where they'd started.

"Are we safe now?" Skyla asked.

They looked around. The walls looked as solid as ever.

"We should be," Coralie said. "I think Blaze only melted the hidden cave."

Blaze's head drooped as she gave a small peep.

"Don't be sad," Skyla said, giving Blaze a hug. "You did a great job!"

Tag showed Blaze the new piece of the Ember Stone. "Look! We couldn't have gotten this without you—and your fire power."

"Peep!" Blaze cried. She danced around the ice cavern.

Tag held up the two warm pieces of the Ember Stone. He could see where they fit together, but there was a large jagged edge where more pieces would fit.

"Let's get out of here," Tag said. "I can't shake the feeling that we're being followed."

"I hope it's not Thorn," Skyla said.

"Who is Thorn?" Coralie asked.

Skyla shuddered. "You don't want to know."

"Thorn is an evil vulture," Tag told Coralie. "He is using dark magic called The Shadow to destroy Perodia. The stone may be the only thing that can stop him."

"I hope I never meet him!" Coralie said.

"We'd better hurry," Skyla said. "Which way should we go?"

"Let's follow the berries," Tag said. "If we pick up every single one, they should lead us back outside."

Skyla grinned. "Good plan!"

"Berries!" Blaze said. She hopped over to pick up a berry in her beak.

Tag led the way along a narrow icy path, dropping berries into his sack as he went.

But soon the friends came face to face with a wall of ice.

"How did berries get here?" Tag muttered. "It's a dead end."

"Lost!" Blaze peeped.

"We're not lost," Tag told her. "We're just . . ."

"Um . . . Tag," Skyla interrupted, tapping Tag on the shoulder.

Tag turned around and gasped.

Two gigantic spotted ice leopards were standing in front of them with a pile of berries at their feet. Their sharp teeth hung down from their huge jaws like icicles.

The ice leopards snarled, digging their hooked claws into the ice. Their eyes flashed bright orange.

Tag gulped. "Thorn's spies!"

"Thorn has spies?!" Coralie squeaked. She covered her eyes with her flippers.

"They must have followed our berries— and then moved them to trap us!" Skyla said, pulling out her slingshot.

Blaze's feathers trembled. Tag moved in front of her.

"We're trapped!" Coralie cried.

TIME FOR BATTLE

GRRRRRRR! The ice leopards growled as they moved closer to the four friends. Tag could feel their hot breath on his feathers.

"Blaze! Coralie! Get behind us!" Tag shouted. He pulled out his dagger.

Skyla stood beside Tag, ready to fight. "Time for battle!" she cried.

Skyla loaded an acorn into her slingshot. Quick as a flash, she shot it into the left eye of one of the leopards.

The leopard fell back and roared.

Skyla reloaded her slingshot and aimed it at the other ice leopard.

The leopard swiped its claws at Tag, but he ducked just in time.

"Stay back!" Tag yelled, waving his dagger at the ice leopard.

Skyla shot another acorn. The ice leopard snarled and slunk back.

GRRRRRRR! The leopards growled. They paced up and down at the end of the path, keeping the four friends penned in on all sides.

"Why aren't they attacking?" Coralie asked.

"They must be waiting for Thorn," Skyla said with a shudder.

We need to find a way out, Tag thought. *I won't let Thorn have the Ember Stone—or Blaze.*

Tag spotted large icicles hanging from the ceiling—right above the ice leopards' heads.

"Blaze," Tag whispered, "can you hit those with your fire power?" He looked up at the icicles.

Blaze eyed the ceiling and nodded.

"You can do this, Blaze," Tag told her. "Just bring down those icicles—don't melt the whole cavern!"

Blaze flapped her wings. Her feathers grew hotter and hotter until small flames appeared.

The ice leopards' jaws dropped. They backed away from Blaze's flaming wings. Blaze aimed at the ceiling.

"Not again!" Skyla yelled, taking cover. Coralie covered her eyes with her flippers.

WHAM!

Fire bolts flew out from Blaze's wings. They hit the icicles.

Tag held his breath. At first, nothing happened.

Finally, there was a loud creak, then a crack. The ice leopards looked up. They yelped as the huge icicles came crashing down!

NO WAY OUT

C RASH!

Large icicles smashed to pieces on the ground, right in front of the ice leopards.

The creatures' eyes glowed orange as they hissed and snarled.

"That made them mad!" Skyla said.

WHAM! WHAM!

Fire bolts shot out from Blaze's feathers and hit the ceiling again. The ice leopards backed away.

Blaze flapped her wings. The flames grew higher. "Peep! Peep!"

A small fire bolt shot past Skyla's ear. She dove to the floor.

"Oh no!" Coralie cried. She stuck her head into a mound of snow.

Another huge fire bolt exploded from Blaze's wings.

There was a loud **CRACK!** Part of the ceiling fell onto the path. Ice and snow blocked the leopards from view.

"Good work, Blaze!" Tag said.

"Peep!" Blaze dropped to the ground. Her wings smoked, but they were no longer on fire.

"Blaze, you did it!" Skyla cheered. "You controlled your power. And Thorn's spies can't reach us!"

But now the four friends were *really* trapped. They were stuck between a huge snow pile and an icy dead end.

Coralie's head popped out from the snow mound. "Now how are we going to escape?"

"Maybe we can dig our way out through this wall?" Tag said.

Skyla shook her head. "The ice is too thick," she said.

"Blaze could melt a hole in it," Coralie suggested.

Blaze lifted her tired wings.

"Blaze has worn herself out," Tag said.

Suddenly, Skyla's ears pricked up. "Do you hear that?" she asked.

Tag listened carefully.

GRRRRRRR! SCRITCH! There was a low growl and a digging sound. Tag turned to the huge snow pile. It was the only thing stopping the ice leopards from getting to his friends—and to the Ember Stone.

"The ice leopards are coming for us!" Tag cried.

CHAPTER 13

ESCAPE

SCRITCH! SCRATCH! The ice leopards scraped and dug at the snow pile with their claws and teeth.

"Do something, Tag!" Skyla cried.

Tag flew to the top of the huge snow pile. Two large orange eyes peered back at him. The ice leopard swiped a paw at Tag.

Tag fell to the ground, knocking open his sack.

Berries, nuts and acorns, and Grey's magical map slid across the ice—along with the two pieces of the Ember Stone!

Skyla picked up the pieces. They were glowing.

"They're still warm," she told the others.

Tag noticed Skyla's paws trembling.

"Are you okay?" Tag asked her.

"It's not me—it's the stones! They're shaking!" Skyla said. She lifted the stones to her ear. "And they're humming!"

"Be careful," Tag warned. "The Ember Stone is filled with powerful magic—who knows what those pieces could do."

Skyla put the pieces on the ground. Tag watched with wide eyes as the stones shook faster and faster. The stones hummed louder and louder, like a thousand buzzing bees.

Suddenly, the two pieces of the Ember Stone slid toward each other. There was a flash of blinding, purple light.

When Tag looked again, there were no longer two pieces of stone, but one.

"Whoa!" Tag said.

"Did you know that would happen?" Skyla asked Blaze.

Blaze shrugged.

"The firehawks *were* the guardians of the Ember Stone," Tag told her. He reached for the stone. "Ouch, it's hot!" He dropped the stone to the ground.

SCRITCH! SCRATCH! Another chunk of snow crumbled off the pile.

"The ice leopards are getting closer," Skyla said. "We have to hurry!"

"Look!" Coralie said, pointing at the stone. It had made a puddle of melted ice.

Tag grinned. "Blaze may be too tired to use her fire power, but we can use the Ember Stone to melt the ice! It must be more powerful now that the two pieces have joined together. Hurry, before it loses heat!"

Skyla frowned. "The stone is too hot to hold . . ."

"Not for a firehawk!" Tag said.

Blaze picked up the Ember Stone in her beak. She held the glowing stone up to the ice wall behind them.

It melted the ice until there was a hole big enough for all of them to fit through. Sunlight shone into the cavern.

"It worked!" Skyla cried as she scurried outside.

Blaze dropped the hot stone into the sack. **FLUMPFFFF!** Snow and ice tumbled down behind them. The two angry ice leopards charged through the snow pile.

"Run!" Tag yelled.

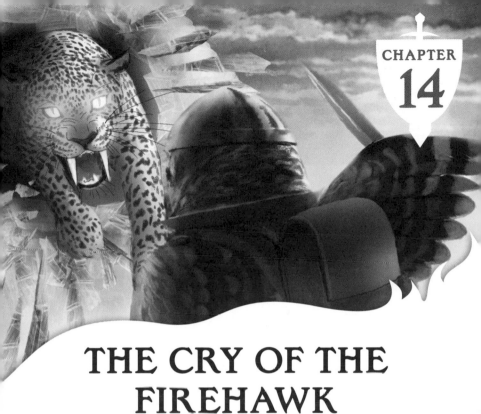

THE CRY OF THE FIREHAWK

Tag reached for his dagger as the leopards leaped through the hole in the wall. One landed right in front of Tag.

Tag could feel the leopard's hot breath on his feathers as the dark creature snapped at his wings.

Skyla shot acorns at the other ice leopard, but they bounced off its thick, spotted fur. Skyla was cornered.

"We're doomed!" Coralie cried. She dove beneath a large mound of snow.

Tag looked at Blaze standing beside him. *I have to keep her safe!* he thought.

But before Tag could do anything, Blaze moved toward the leopards.

"SKRAAA!" Blaze cried. Her wings glowed as she ran at the ice leopards.

The leopards yelped and fell to the ground as Blaze screeched again.

"SKRAAAAA!"

The ice leopards' icy teeth shattered. They broke into hundreds of tiny pieces that fell onto the snow beneath their paws. The leopards scrambled to their feet and ran away.

"That was awesome!" a voice boomed behind them.

Tag, Skyla, and Blaze turned around.

Gilbert stood on a snow mound, clapping his flippers together.

Another seal popped his head out of the snow—then another, and another.

"You did it, Blaze," Tag said. "Your cry saved us!"

"Coralie? Is that you?" A seal shuffled across the ice to where Coralie hid beneath the snow.

"Mama?" Coralie cried, as she lifted her head from the snow.

The seals hugged each other.

"My baby!" Coralie's mom cried.

Gilbert turned to Tag. "We can't thank you enough. If you and your friends ever need help, the seals are on your side." He pointed a flipper to the black, cracked ice. "We've seen the damage Thorn can do."

"Come visit us again," Coralie told her new friends.

The friends said good-bye and the seals settled down beneath their snow mounds.

Tag checked their supplies.

"Blaze's fire power isn't a secret anymore," Skyla said. "Now Thorn will be even more determined to find Blaze—and the Ember Stone."

"We'll have to move faster than ever to stay ahead," Tag replied.

Blaze pulled Grey's map from the sack. She dropped it at Tag's feet. "Peep!"

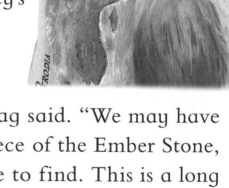

"Yes, Blaze," Tag said. "We may have found a second piece of the Ember Stone, but there are more to find. This is a long journey."

"Where to next?" Skyla asked.

Tag laid the map flat on the ground. He placed the still-warm and slightly-bigger Ember Stone on top of it.

A bright spot appeared. "Whispering Oak," Tag read.

Skyla pointed to the map. "It's not going to be easy to cross the Shifting Sands," she said.

"Together, we can do it," Tag replied. "We have to save Perodia."

"Peep!" Blaze said, smiling.

Tag looked to the west. "Our adventure continues."

ABOUT THE AUTHOR

KATRINA CHARMAN has wanted to be a children's book writer ever since she was eleven, when her teacher asked her class to write an epilogue to Roald Dahl's *Matilda*. Katrina's teacher thought her writing was good enough to send to Roald Dahl himself! Sadly, she never got a reply, but this experience ignited her love of reading and writing. Katrina lives in England with her husband and three daughters. The Last Firehawk is her first early chapter book series in the US.

ABOUT THE ILLUSTRATOR

JEREMY NORTON is an accomplished illustrator and artist who uses digital media to develop images and ideas on screen with light. He was an imaginative and prolific artist as a child, and he still tries to convey that same sense of wonder in his work. Jeremy lives in Spain. The Last Firehawk is his first early chapter book series with Scholastic.

Questions and Activities

1. **R**eread page 7. Why doesn't fire hurt Blaze?

2. **I**s it difficult or easy for Tag and his friends to get the Ember Stone out of the ice wall? Explain.

3. **L**ook at the pictures and words on pages 78-79. What is happening?

4. **W**hat happens when Blaze screeches at the ice leopards?

5. **S**kyla is always ready to use her slingshot! How does she use it to protect her friends? Write a paragraph using examples from the book.